It Shouldn't
Happen to a Frog

It Shouldn't Happen to a Frog

and other stories

Catherine Storr

Illustrated by
Priscilla Lamont

PICCOLO BOOKS

First published 1984 in the *Flying Carpets* series by
Macmillan Children's Books
This Piccolo edition published 1987 by Pan Books Ltd,
Cavaye Place, London SW10 9PG
9 8 7 6 5 4 3 2 1
Text © Catherine Storr 1984
ISBN 0 330 29510 1

Printed and bound in Great Britain by
Cox & Wyman Ltd, Reading

Contents

Frog Prince

"If I'd been the princess in that story, the Frog Prince, I wouldn't have thrown him against the wall. I think that was cruel," Lisa said.

"Then he wouldn't have turned into a handsome prince," her mother said.

"I'd rather have a frog than a prince," Lisa said.

★　　★　　★

SHE WAS PLAYING IN THE GARDEN with the golden ball that was so precious she wasn't often allowed to take it out of the palace. "It's real gold, it's worth a great deal of money.

You must be very careful of it and don't ever lose it," the King her father had told her. Solid gold is extremely heavy, and Lisa couldn't throw the ball up in the air. Mostly she just rolled it across the grass, and tried to guess where it would stop.

This time it stopped just by the marble rim of the fountain. Lisa sat by the fountain and looked down into the water. Orange and golden fish swam past. Sometimes one came almost up to the surface and gaped at her with its fishy mouth. From the dolphin statue in the middle of the fountain the water fell, tinkling, into the pool below. Tinkle, tinkle. Splash, splash. It was very hot and very peaceful there under the trees. Lisa yawned. She was half asleep.

Suddenly there was a louder splash. Drops of water flew up and sprinkled Lisa's face. On the surface of the rippling water, circles grew larger and larger, spreading across to the further side of the pool. The golden ball had rolled over the marble rim and had fallen in.

8

Lisa looked down into the water. She couldn't see anything in that dark green, ferny, fishy world. More drops fell into the water. Lisa's tears. She had been told not to play with the golden ball too near the fountain, she had forgotten and now she had lost it. The King would be cross. No wonder Lisa cried.

She was still crying, five minutes later, when a voice, small and rather hoarse, said, 'Princess!'

Lisa opened her wet eyes and saw, on the fountain's rim, a frog. He was green, with dark stripes down his back. His little froggy hands were spread out on the white marble and his glistening froggy eyes were fixed on her.

"You've lost your golden ball," the frog said.

"Mama will punish me," Lisa sobbed.

"Your father won't be pleased either. It's right down at the bottom of the pool. You'll never be able to get at it," the frog said.

Lisa sobbed louder than ever.

"But I could get it back for you, and your mother and father would never know you'd let it fall into the fountain," the frog said.

Lisa said, "Could you really?" She stopped crying.

"I could. The question is, would I?"

"Please, dear frog. Please fetch it for me," Lisa said.

"I will, if you'll promise me something," the frog said.

Lisa opened her mouth to say, "Of course I'll promise." Then she remembered the silly promises people in fairy stories often made. "I'll give you the first thing I meet on my way home," they said. Or, "I'll give you half of the thing I love most." Then when it came to keeping the promise, they found they had promised to give away their babies, or to split their new brides or bridegrooms in half. So she said carefully, "What do you want me to promise?"

"I want you to take me into the palace and put me on the royal table at meal-times," the frog said.

"Go on," Lisa said, as the frog stopped.

"I want to eat with you off your golden plate."

"Go on."

"I want to drink with you out of your golden cup," the frog said.

"Go on."

"I want to sleep with you in your golden bed." He stopped again.

"Go on."

"That's all," the frog said.

"You don't want my first baby? When I have one," Lisa asked.

"Good grief, no! What would I do with a human baby? Nasty noisy things."

"You don't want half the kingdom? Or half my husband?"

"Certainly not. I wouldn't know where to put them," the frog said.

"Then I'll promise," Lisa said. She had hardly spoken the words, before the frog had disappeared, diving neatly into the water without a splash. A moment later he was back again, holding between his froggy

hands Lisa's golden ball.

"Now, pick me up and carry me into the palace," he ordered. He hopped on to Lisa's palm, and she went back into the palace, carrying the golden ball in one hand and the cool, damp frog in the other.

Presently the Queen looked down the royal table, set with the midday meal. "What's that you have by your plate, my child?" she asked.

"It's a frog, Mama," Lisa answered.

"A frog!" the Queen said, her voice squeaky with surprise.

"He's a very kind frog, Mama. He helped me with something I was doing in the

garden," Lisa said.

"A frog!" the Queen said again, and the King who was a little deaf, said, "What's that? A dog?"

"Eating off our daughter's plate," the Queen said.

"Oh no! Can't have dogs licking plates. It's not hygienic, really it isn't," the King said.

"It's not a dog, it's a frog," Lisa said loudly across the table.

"A frog? Why choose a frog?"

"In any case, it has got to stop. We can't have garden animals on the royal table," the Queen said.

"But, mama, I promised. You always say princesses shouldn't break their promises. I said he could eat off my plate and drink out of my cup," Lisa said. She thought that she had better not mention that the frog would also be sharing her bed.

"Well! I suppose if you promised . . . But when you've finished your meal you must put it back in the garden," the Queen said.

Lisa said, "Yes, Mama," but she thought to herself, "I will tomorrow. I can't yet, not until he's shared my bed once, anyway."

She managed to smuggle the frog into her pocket and carried him about for the rest of the day. But when she got up to her bedroom that night and took him out, the frog was in a bad temper.

"What disgusting food you have. Is that the best the King's cooks can provide?" he asked.

"Roast chicken and peas. Strawberries and ice cream. What was wrong?" Lisa asked.

"Tasteless. Boring. Dead," the frog said.

"What do you mean, dead? What do you like eating, then?"

The frog considered. "Flies. Mosquitoes. Long juicy worms that wriggle as you swallow them. None of your food wriggled. It's so dull! When you plan meals, does no one pay any attention to twitch and squirm? They're quite as important as taste."

"I don't think they do," Lisa said.

"And the water! So clear I could see right through it! Don't you ever have good thick pond water, full of small writhing . . .

things? 'Oh for a beaker full of the warm South, Alive with squirmers, that's the sort I mean . . .' Poetry. You wouldn't appreciate it," the frog said.

"It was you who suggested eating off my

plate and drinking out of my cup," Lisa reminded him.

"Perhaps tomorrow's meals will be different? A caterpillar or two in the cabbage?

Preferably alive, not cooked to a mush?"

"If there are, you can have mine," Lisa said.

"Great! And now to bed. Hop in," the frog said, acting on his own advice. Lisa had hoped that he would be content to sleep on her pillow, but he insisted on getting right into the bed. When the Queen came to kiss her goodnight, Lisa was grateful for this, but later on she regretted it.

The frog was exceedingly restless. First he explored the bed to discover where he wanted to sleep, but after ten minutes he changed his mind and tried another, better spot. During the night he woke Lisa continually, complaining that she was in danger of squashing him, that he was too hot, that he was hungry, or to ask the time.

Early in the morning he hopped round the room in search of flies. When Lisa got up she was more tired than when she had gone to bed, and the frog was irritable. He had a quick swim in the golden basin, and came out congratulating himself on having cooled down at last.

"If you don't like being warm, you shouldn't have asked to sleep in my bed," Lisa said.

"Wouldn't you like to come and share the fountain pool with me?" the frog suggested.

"No thank you. I might drown."

"I could teach you to swim. I might even be able to catch you a dragonfly."

"I don't eat dragonflies."

The frog sighed. His green body puffed out and shrank again. "Then, Princess, I am afraid we are going to have to separate. Our tastes are quite incompatible . . ."

"What does that mean?" Lisa asked.

"Means we don't enjoy the same things."

"No, we don't," Lisa said.

"Sad though it seems, I think we shall have to go our separate ways. You to your palace, with the horrible food

and the over-heated beds. I to my nourishing and calming pool."

"All right," Lisa said.

"I am sorry. It just hasn't worked out. I hope we part without any hard feelings," said the frog.

"I'm sorry too. I'd always wanted to have a frog as a pet," Lisa said. She saw immediately that she had said the wrong thing.

"A pet! A PET! Is that what you think of me, the top frog of the fountain? You stupid little girl! Don't you know a Frog Prince when you meet one? I am heir to a fabulous kingdom. If things had gone as they should, I intended to marry you, to make you my queen! And you have the insolence to talk about me as a pet!"

"I'm sorry!" Lisa called after him, as the frog indignantly plopped on to the floor and

21

made his way out of the room. Lisa ran after him.

"Please don't be offended! I didn't mean . . . I didn't want to hurt your feelings . . . I like frogs! I really do! . . ."

But the frog was hurrying down the great staircase. Plop! Plop! Plop! on each step, leaving wet marks on the crimson carpet. At the bottom he turned his head to say, "And next time you drop something into my fountain, you can frogging well get it yourself." With that he hopped out of the open palace door and disappeared. Lisa got back into bed. She had had a very short night. But before she went back to sleep, she thought, "Perhaps frogs don't really make very good pets. Perhaps that's why the princess in the story was pleased when hers turned into a handsome young prince. Only I don't want a prince either. Not yet . . ."

And then she was asleep.

The Three Bears

"I wouldn't have eaten any of the porridge," Lisa said.

"What porridge?"

"The porridge Goldilocks found in the bears' house. I'd have left all the bowls just as they were on the table," Lisa said.

"I've always wondered how they managed that one bowl was too hot to eat and the next one was too cold," her mother said.

"What I don't understand is why did they go out for a walk when their breakfast was just ready?" Lisa said.

★　　★　　★

BUT WHEN SHE FOUND HERSELF WALKING THROUGH THE DOOR into the bears' kitchen, she did understand. There were the bowls of porridge on the table, one huge, one middling-sized, one tiny. The huge one was steaming hot; no one could possibly have eaten it. Obviously the Father bear had said, "I can't eat this, it's far too hot to touch. Let's go for a stroll in the forest, and I'll have it when we get back."

The oatmealy smell coming from the huge bowl reminded Lisa that she didn't much care for porridge. She looked around for something else to eat.

Near the fireplace was a large wooden cupboard. It was too high up for Lisa to reach without standing on something. She looked at the huge big chair at the head of the table and pushed it with her foot. It shifted an inch or two, but it was far too heavy for her to drag right across to the cupboard. She tried the middling-sized chair. She could just move it, but it was still uncomfortably heavy. She turned to the smallest chair and managed to get it right up to the cupboard. Then she climbed up and, standing on the seat of the chair, she opened the cupboard door.

On the shelves inside were many things just like those Lisa's mother had in her kitchen cupboard: flour, sugar, salt, tea. Oats, of course. And jars and jars of honey and tins and tins of syrup. There was a tin labelled BISCUITS. Lisa looked inside it hopefully, but it was empty. There was a round cake tin in the top far corner which Lisa could nearly, but not quite, reach. She stood on tiptoe and leaned forward so that her fingers just touched the bottom of the tin, and as she did so, the little chair tipped under her feet and Lisa fell off it on to the floor.

As she sat there, rubbing her shoulder, which was bruised, she saw with dismay that the back of the little chair had come away from the seat and that one of its legs had broken right off. What was equally bad was that Lisa had fallen across the table. The smallest bowl of porridge was lying in pieces on the floor and there was a distressing mess of porridge on the table, rapidly dripping down to join another mess on the floor.

"I'd better get out quick!" Lisa thought, and she ran to the door. But when she looked round it, she saw, not far away, three figures coming towards the cottage from the wood.

There was a great huge figure, a middling-sized figure, and a small little tiny figure skipping around. The three bears were coming back for their breakfast.

There was nowhere in the kitchen for Lisa to hide in or behind. The only place she could escape to was up the stairs; so that was where Lisa went. Just in time. She could hear the squeals of the small little tiny bear as he came jumping along the path leading up to the front door.

Lisa looked desperately round the room in which she now found herself. There was a great huge bed, much too high for her to

climb up to. There was a small little bed, with its bedclothes still in a huddle. Quick as lightning, Lisa jumped into this little bed, and tried to make herself as flat as she could.

From downstairs she could hear the gruff voice of the huge big bear.

"Someone's been in here while we were out," it said.

"Someone's moved my bowl of porridge," said a not-so-deep, furrier voice. It was true, Lisa had just touched the middling-sized bowl to make sure it was cold, as the story says.

"Someone's spilt my porridge all over the place and they've broken the bowl too," said a squeaky little voice. That, of course, was the little tiny bear.

"Someone's moved my chair from the head of the table," said the deep gruff voice.

"Someone's moved my chair too. I didn't leave it half across the room like that," said the furry voice, disapprovingly.

"Someone's been throwing my chair about and broken it so I can't sit in it any more," said the small squeaky voice, not sounding exactly sad about it.

"I'll mend your chair, my boy, don't worry about that," said the deep gruff voice.

"I'll make you some more porridge," said the furry voice.

"Mumma, can't I have biscuits and honey instead of porridge? Just for once?" the squeaky voice begged.

"We'd better have a look around and see who's been here," the deep gruff voice said, sounding nearer to Lisa. Could they be coming up the stairs?

"Come and eat your breakfast first. It's always the same. Just as soon as I put the food on the table, you think of something you've got to do that very minute, and then it gets cold and you complain about that," said the furry voice, scolding. Lisa heard chairs being pulled up to the table. She heard the sounds of

chomping. Chump, swallow. Chump, chump, swallow. For a long time no one spoke. Lisa lay very still. Perhaps the bears would go for another walk after their meal, and then she would be able to escape.

She heard two chairs pushed back from the table. She heard a satisfied, deep belch. "Very good porridge, my dear, even if it had cooled down a trifle too much. Now let's look for whoever it was who came in here while we were out," the deep gruff voice said.

"Perhaps it was a goblin," the little squeaky voice said.

"Don't be silly, Teeny-Tiny. There's no such thing as a goblin."

"Perhaps it was a mouse."

"Oh dear! I hope not. I'm frightened of mice," the furry voice said.

"Now you're being stupid, my dear. A great, middling-sized, grown-up mother bear, frightened of mice?" the deep gruff voice said.

"They scuttle so," the furry voice said, apologetically.

"Don't tell me it was a mouse that broke Teeny-Tiny's chair."

"Teeny-Tiny, will you go upstairs for Mumma and fetch her a hankie?" the furry voice purred. Lisa heard steps coming up the stairs towards the bedroom. But Teeny-Tiny did not go to look for his mother's handkerchief. Instead he came directly over to the little bed and pulled the blankets back. He and Lisa looked at each other.

"You're not Goldilocks! Your hair is quite brown," the smallest bear said.

"How do you know about Goldilocks?" Lisa asked.

"Everyone knows about Goldilocks. Who are you?"

"I'm Lisa. I'm terribly sorry about your porridge. . ."

"That's all right. I hate porridge," the smallest bear said.

"But I broke your bowl. . ."

"If I haven't got a bowl,
Mumma can't make me eat porridge," the smallest bear said.

"And I broke your dear little chair. . ."

"It's too small. It's been too small for ages.
The trouble is that Mumma wants to keep me
a baby, so everything I have has to be teeny-
tiny. It's terrible."

From down below the furry voice floated
up the stairs. "Hurry up, Teeny-Tiny. I want
my handkerchief, I need to blow my nose."

"Coming at once, Mumma bear!" the
smallest bear called back. To Lisa he said,

33

"You'd better get out before they start coming upstairs to look for you. You can get out of the window and climb down the tree outside. I've often done it while they're asleep. I'll make sure they aren't looking out of the window."

Lisa clambered out on to the window-sill. As the littlest bear had said there was a convenient, ancient mulberry tree, asking to be climbed down, just below her. "Thank you," she said to the smallest bear.

"Any time. Come back and wreck my horrible little bed," he said. But as she ran away through the wood, Lisa thought she probably wouldn't ever go back. Here she was, running away, after escaping by the bedroom window, just as Goldilocks had. She hadn't been any cleverer, in spite of knowing the story beforehand. "Perhaps it's especially difficult with bears," Lisa thought.

Bluebeard

"I think Bluebeard's wife was stoo-oopid," Lisa said, shutting the book of fairy tales.

"Why? Because she married a man who'd had six wives before?" her mum asked.

"I expect she thought she'd be different. And perhaps she liked men with beards, especially when they were as rich as he was."

"Why was she stupid, then?"

"To go and look in the secret room. After all, he had warned her not to."

"Don't you think that was probably why she did? If Bluebeard hadn't mentioned that room, she might never have thought about it again."

*   *   *

AND THAT WAS HOW IT WAS IN BLUE-BEARD'S CASTLE. After Bluebeard had gone off on his mysterious journey, Lisa couldn't stop looking at the bunch of keys he had handed to her, with the strict instructions that she should guard them well until his return.

He had hardly disappeared down the long road that led up to the castle, before Lisa and her sister Anne had begun to explore all the rooms which were opened by the big keys. They

looked at rooms full of furniture, rooms full of pictures, rooms full of tapestries, of gold, of silver, of jewellery. "Too much of everything. Fancy having to keep all that clean!" Anne said.

"I don't have to. Bluebeard told me all he wanted me to do was to enjoy myself," Lisa said.

"Are you enjoying yourself?" Anne asked.

"Not much. I'm bored, looking at all that stuff. It isn't much use, really, is it? I mean, it was fun at first, dressing up and trying on those necklaces and crowns and things, but I don't want to go on doing it all day."

"Let's go and swing in the garden."

"Swinging makes me giddy."

"Let's dress Tomkins up in pearls and things. He'd be terribly grand. After all, cats don't generally get to wear real diamonds and pearls."

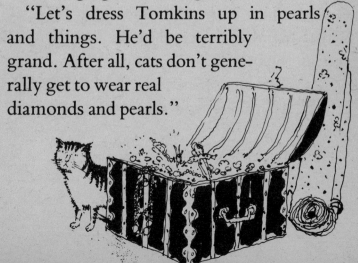

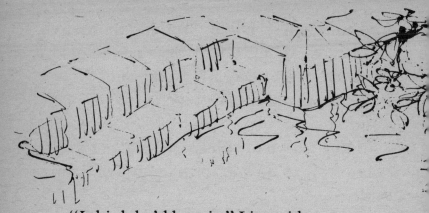

"I think he'd hate it," Lisa said.

"Well, go on then. You suggest something."

Lisa tried hard to think of something she really wanted to do. But there wasn't anything. Or rather, the thing she really wanted to do was exactly what she had been warned against. She wanted to see what was inside the locked room at the end of the long corridor, which would be opened by the little key, the last on the bunch.

"Let's go and swim in the pool," she said.

"There was a frog there this morning," Anne said.

"I don't mind. I quite like frogs."

"I don't."

"I'm going there, anyway," Lisa said. She went down the grand marble staircase to the garden, where the pool, also built of marble, lay surrounded by orange trees. You could float on the green water and pick oranges from the long branches that leaned over the pool. It didn't matter if eating the fruit made you sticky, because you could wash your fingers in the stream that ran, all the time, through the pool. Lisa had never met another pool anything like as good.

She had been swimming there for about ten minutes, before Anne came to join her. After they had come out of the pool, and were sitting drying their hair in the sun, Lisa asked, "What were you doing just now?"

Anne said, "Nothing special," in the voice which tells you that you are not hearing the truth.

"What d'you mean, nothing?"

"Nothing important."

Lisa looked hard at her sister. "You didn't go into that secret room?"

"Of course not. How could I? You've got the key."

Lisa leant over and felt in the pocket of the enormously grand skirt she had to wear as Bluebeard's wife. It was lying on the warm marble by her side. To her relief, the huge bunch of keys was still there, bulging out the stiff silk. She pulled it out, and gazed at the little key she had been forbidden to use.

She separated it from the others and showed it to Anne. "Look! It's got a mark on it. It's sort of red."

"Blood!" Anne said.

"Don't be silly. It's rust."

"Are you going to try to get it off?"

"Why should I? If I cleaned it up too much Bluebeard might think there was something suspicious about it."

Anne sighed. "I do wish we knew what he keeps in that little room."

"How do you know it's a little room?" Lisa asked.

"I was just walking along that corridor and looking at the other doors. They're all much bigger than *that* one, and there's hardly any room between the last of them – that's the one where we found all those furs – and the bathroom in the sort of turret thing."

"It's probably a cupboard where they keep brooms and things," Lisa said.

"It's dark enough for a cupboard," Anne said.

"Anne! You did look inside!"

"Only through the keyhole. I couldn't see anything."

There was a pause.

"If we had a really long ladder, we could look in through the window," Anne said.

"I'm not sure there is a window. When we were in the garden yesterday I counted the windows on that side of the castle, and the bathroom window in the little turret thing is next to the last room we went into. Anyway, we haven't got a long ladder."

"Perhaps that's why it was so dark. The secret room, I mean," Anne said.

Lisa shivered.

"The sun's gone behind that big tree. Let's go up to the top of the tower and have a picnic lunch. If we're up there I don't have to wear that dress all the time. It's terribly heavy and it scratches me."

"It wouldn't be so heavy if you hadn't borrowed that gold belt to wear with it."

"But it's so beautiful! I love all the rubies and emeralds and things on the buckle."

They picked up their clothes and made their way back into the castle. "We'll have to take everything up with us in case anyone comes to call this afternoon. I'm sure Bluebeard would be furious if his visitors saw you in a bikini," Anne said, as they climbed the narrow winding staircase that led to the top of the tower.

"Aren't the boys coming over this afternoon?" Lisa said.

"They said so. They wanted to come here to see the castle one day while Bluebeard's away. They think he's guessed they tried to persuade you not to marry him, and that's why he's not very polite to them."

"Brothers can't prevent their sister from marrying someone. . . ." Lisa had begun, when noises from below interrupted her. She ran to the parapet to look down. The courtyard was filling with clattering horses and shouting men, and at the head of the troop she saw Bluebeard himself on his magnificent black charger.

"Quick! Help me to get dressed. I'll have to go down to greet him. I wonder why he didn't stay till the end of the week? He's come back two days early."

She dressed as quickly as she could. But Bluebeard was already calling for her, before she had reached the great hall on the ground floor. He caught her in his arms and kissed her. He told her that he loved her so much he couldn't bear to be away from her for another hour. "Did you miss me?" he asked, and Lisa said "Yes." But it wasn't true. She realized now that it had been more fun playing with Anne than being grand and proper as Blue-beard's wife.

"Has everything gone well in my absence?" Bluebeard asked, sitting in his large gilded chair and looking at her keenly.

"Yes, everything has gone very well," Lisa answered.

"Good. So now, Madam, give me back my

keys."

Lisa pulled the great bunch of keys out of her pocket and handed it to Bluebeard. He examined it closely. He went through the keys, one by one until he reached the last and the smallest. It was the key of the secret room. Bluebeard held it close to his eyes, then suddenly shouted.

"There is a stain on this key! So, Madam, you disobeyed my orders and visited the secret chamber! Are you aware, that the punishment for disobedience is death?" he cried. Somehow this speech did not sound quite right. It sounded almost as if Bluebeard had learned the words by heart and had said them so often that he had forgotten what they meant.

"No, I didn't. I didn't go into that room, and the stain's rust. It was there when you gave me the keys," Lisa said.

"Do not lie to me, Madam. You opened the door of the forbidden chamber, and when you saw what was within, you were so startled that the key dropped from your hand and became stained with blood," Bluebeard went on as if he hadn't heard her.

"Why should there have been any blood around? Anyway, if I had gone there, which I didn't, and I had dropped the key in it, I'd have washed it off before you came back," Lisa said.

Bluebeard's hand, which had been on the hilt of his sword, dropped to his side.

"You mean you really did not open the last door with this little key?" he asked.

"Really I didn't."

"All my former wives unlocked that door."

"So it is true that you've had other wives! I wouldn't believe that story before we got

married. What happened to them?" Lisa said.

Bluebeard did not answer this question. He said, "That makes it very awkward."

"What's awkward?" Lisa asked.

Bluebeard hesitated. Then he said, "Well, you see it's like this. I like getting married, but I don't like staying married for long. So I discovered that if I told my wives that they must never open that secret door, and that if they did I would have to kill them, they always did what they'd been told not to. Then I had to kill them, and that left me free for the next wife. I was sure you'd do what the others did and so. . ."

He stopped, as a well-dressed young woman came running into the hall. She ran up to Bluebeard and threw her arms round him. "Darling Bluebeard, it's a fantastic castle. Of course I'll be your wife. Let's get married at once. Why not this afternoon?" she said.

"He can't marry you. He's married to me," Lisa said.

"You! You're only a scruffy little girl," the young woman said, not letting go of Bluebeard, who said angrily, "You were supposed to wait outside until I . . . until I sent for you."

"You'd better think again about marrying him. He's just been explaining to me that he doesn't keep any of his wives very long. I'm probably the seventh, or it may be the eighth or ninth, and now he's trying to think up a good excuse for killing me off so that he can marry you," Lisa said.

"Execute her for telling these horrible lies about you," the young woman said to Bluebeard, without

taking her eyes off him.

"That's a brilliant idea. Take your arms away, dearest, so that I can draw my sword."

"Only make her take off that dress first. It's just what I've been looking for, and it would be a pity to get it covered with blood, wouldn't it?" the young woman said.

"Give me five minutes, and I'll change into something more suitable," Lisa said, and escaped towards the stairway to the tower. She ran up as fast as she could and found Anne still lazily sunning herself on the flat roof at the top.

"What was all that shouting down below?" Anne asked.

"I haven't got time to explain. Bluebeard's going to kill me because I didn't . . . because he wants . . . Anne! Look down the road while I'm taking off my dress. Are our brothers coming? They might be able to save me."

Anne went to the parapet and looked out. "No. There's no one."

From down below came a roar from Bluebeard. "Madam, come down! You must have

changed your dress by now."

"Anne, look again. Isn't that a cloud of dust on the road?"

"Yes. And . . . no, it's only a flock of sheep."

"Madam, if you will not come down to me, I shall come up to you," shouted Bluebeard at the bottom of the stairs.

"Our brothers never arrive on time. They're always late for appointments," Anne remarked.

Lisa made up her mind.

"That's right. It's no good waiting for them. I'll let Bluebeard come up the stairs. You stand over there by the parapet where he can see you, and when he's got to the top, you say, 'Hi, Bluebeard, are you looking for something?' so that you get his attention. Then, while he's looking at you, I'll hit him on the head with my gold belt. I should think that would probably make him fall down quite a lot of steps, and it might give us a chance to escape. If we're lucky he might break an arm or a leg or something so that he couldn't run after us."

Bluebeard came panting up the stairs. He was not used to taking exercise, and by the time he had reached the roof, he was quite out of breath. Anne hardly needed to speak to him, he was already unprepared for Lisa's attack. The jewel-studded buckle of the gold belt hit him hard between the eyes. He stepped back, lost his footing, and fell. Lisa and Anne heard his heavy body tumbling down the stairwell. A long, long way. Then there was silence.

Lisa was just beginning to say, "I wonder if he's . . ." when Anne cried out, "There's another cloud of dust on the road! Two horsemen!

It's our brothers come to save us. At last!"

The brothers, aware that they were much later than they should have been, wasted no time once they were in the castle. Finding a beautiful young lady in tears and Bluebeard lying unconscious on the floor, they immediately, without asking any questions, hacked him to death with their swords.

Later, when they had had the situation explained, they protested the Bluebeard had in any case deserved to die, that he had been only half alive when they found him and after such a fall he could have sur-

vived only as a helpless cripple. Quite soon they were congratulating themselves on having saved him from further suffering and also on having made Lisa his widow, possessed of countless riches. They expected that in her gratitude, Lisa would wish to share some of these riches with them. Meanwhile both brothers were prepared to try to console the weeping young woman.

★   ★   ★

Very much later, when they were back in their own home, Anne said to Lisa, "I wonder what there really was in the secret little room."

"Didn't I tell you? After all the fuss was over, I went and had a look."

"Was it all bloody and full of dead wives?"

"Of course not. They'd have smelled, wouldn't they? Nothing like that."

"What was it, then?"

"Bottles. Heaps of bottles. No, not that

sort. Bottles of hair dye. Blue. And mirrors all round the walls. Aren't men extraordinary?"

"I do see why he had to keep that room locked," Anne said.

Cinderella

TO BEGIN WITH everything happened exactly as Lisa had expected. Her stepmother made her do all the nastiest jobs around the house, never bought her any new clothes, and scolded her most of the time. One of her stepsisters was downright ugly, and the other one was plain. Lisa-Cinderella was a great deal prettier than either of them, even when she was dressed in rags and had got her hands and face dirty from scrubbing the floor and raking out the fire.

The invitation to the ball at the palace

arrived, just as she had known it would. The stepsisters ordered themselves splendid new ball gowns, and pranced around in them, admiring themselves. They pretended to be sorry for Lisa-Cinderella because there was no chance of her being allowed to go to the palace with them, but Lisa knew quite well that when they said, "What a pity you haven't any clothes and can't come with us", they were really feeling pleased with themselves for being so much grander and luckier than she was.

After everyone else had gone off to the ball, Lisa-Cinderella sat by the fire and waited for her fairy godmother to arrive. To save time, she fetched the pumpkin which was going to turn into a coach, and the trap with the fat grey rat and the smaller trap which held four very frightened mice. So, when the godmother finally appeared, stepping neatly into the kitchen through the fireplace as if it had been a door, Lisa was all ready for her.

"Dear, dear! What's all this? Everyone gone off to the ball and left you alone in the kitchen?" the fairy godmother said. She looked round the kitchen, then said suddenly to Lisa, "Why aren't you crying?"

"I was just going to," Lisa said.

"Perhaps you don't want to go to the ball? You'd rather stay here?"

"No! I do want to go to the ball. I was just hoping you'd be coming to help me," Lisa said.

The godmother frowned. "You shouldn't take people for granted. I didn't have to come and help you. It was purely out of the goodness of my heart."

"It's very good of you," Lisa said, as gratefully as she could.

"Very well. So you wish to go to the ball."

The godmother looked round the kitchen again and then asked sharply, "Why do you keep those traps in here? You shouldn't have rats and mice in the kitchen, it's not hygienic."

Lisa did not want to offend the old lady by seeming to know too much about the magic she was going to do. She said, "It's lonely here without anyone to talk to. I brought the rat and the mice in here for company." She felt it was an unlikely explanation, and she wasn't surprised when the godmother snorted.

Fortunately, however, the old lady did not waste any time with further questions. Taking out her wand, she quickly transformed the pumpkin into a coach, the rat into a stout coachman, and the four mice into four lively horses. There was one nasty moment when the rat and the mice had been taken out

of their traps, and were still rattish and mouseish, before they had taken on more acceptable shapes.

Finally the godmother touched Lisa's rags with her wand, and she stood there, in a ball gown which glimmered and shone. When Lisa lifted the heavy skirts which swept the floor, she saw, to her satisfaction, the famous pair of glass slippers.

"Now, be off with you! And don't forget! At midnight, my magic loses its power. The coach will become a pumpkin again, the coachman and horses will turn back into vermin, and your splendid dress will be rags. So you had better get back here in good time," the godmother said, stepping back into the fireplace and disappearing among the dying flames.

The ball was wonderful. Very sparkly and glittery. There were a great many beautiful ladies, wearing beautiful clothes, but after Lisa–Cinderella had arrived, the Prince had eyes for no one but her. He eagerly engaged

her for the next dance. "If I could choose, I would dance with no one but you. But my royal parents may insist that I sometimes dance with some of the princesses and duchesses who have done me the honour of coming to the ball," he said.

Sure enough, after he had danced twice with Lisa, the Prince did have several other partners. Lisa quite understood that a young prince must do his duty by his guests. In fact, not having to dance was quite a relief, because

although the ball was perfect in every other way, the dances were not comfortable. The trouble was that they were all formal dances which Lisa had never learned, and she hadn't any idea of what she was supposed to be doing.

Her partners – for she had many besides the Prince – were as helpful as possible. "Take my hand and make a circle round me," they said. "Join hands with that lady and skip down between the people standing and clapping." "Curtsey when I bow." "Thread your way in and out of the gentlemen and ladies holding hands." But though she tried to follow their instructions, poor Lisa was always finding

herself bumping into this gentleman, or trip-
ping over that lady's feet, or the only person
in the ballroom to be standing still while the
others skipped around. She seemed to have
spent her time in saying "I'm so sorry!",
"Excuse me!", "I beg your pardon." So she
was pleased when the Prince seemed happy
just to sit by her, telling her how lovely she
was, or to take her down to supper, and ply
her with delicious food and drink.

But in spite of enjoying herself so much,
Lisa did not forget her godmother's warning.
At a quarter to twelve – midnight – she
thanked the Prince warmly, left the ballroom,

found her coach with the stout coachman and the four horses, and was safely carried back to her own house. Just as she had got back inside, she heard the church clock strike midnight. Sure enough, her fine dress immediately disappeared, and when she looked out of the back door, she saw the pumpkin lying in the gutter and heard the delighted squeaks of the rat and the mice as they escaped down the road.

The only things left to remind her of the evening's gaiety were the glass slippers. Lisa-Cinderella hid them under the bed, and went to sleep, congratulating herself on having been much cleverer than the real Cinderella, who hadn't remembered to get home in time.

The next morning, her stepmother and her

sisters wanted to tell her all about the ball. How the Prince had admired them. How he had danced with each of the sisters. How they had each hoped that she might be the lucky girl he was going to choose for his bride. Until there had appeared a wonderful lady, in a dress made of sunshine and moonbeams, who had stolen the Prince's heart. Before the end of the festivities, after the lady had left, the Prince had publicly announced that he meant to marry this unknown beauty, if he had to search for her to the ends of the earth.

"That's all right. He'll go round with the glass slipper, trying it on all the girls he can find, and it won't fit any of them. But when he comes here, after the ugly sisters have tried to squeeze their horrible great feet into the slipper he's got, I'll come out from the kitchen . . ."

This was the moment when Lisa realized what she had done. Or rather, what she had *not* done.

She had not left one of the glass slippers behind for the Prince to find. Both slippers were upstairs, underneath her bed. So how was the Prince going to recognize the beautiful lady he had fallen in love with at the Palace ball?

This time, after her stepmother and sisters had taken themselves off to visit their friends, to boast about their triumphs at the ball, Lisa sat again by the kitchen fire, and this time she cried and her tears were real.

"Crying again? Never mind! You *shall* go to the ball, my dear. I can't manage a coach this time, but if you could find me a couple of curtain rings and a bit of chain . . . any sort of chain. Off a lavatory cistern, if you like . . . I'm sure I could whip you up a bicycle," her fairy godmother was saying. Lisa saw her unfurl her wand and look hopefully round the kitchen.

"No, it's not the ball. I mean . . . there isn't another ball. It's the glass slippers. I've got . . ."

"I know you only have one, just now, my dear. But don't worry! Before long the Prince

66

will be along with the other, and then you'll try it on, and it will fit you, and . . ."

"It isn't that! I've got them both. Two slippers!" Lisa said.

"You have *two* slippers?" the godmother said, in an awful tone.

"You see, I came home before midnight. Like you said," Lisa said.

The old lady made the noise with her tongue which is generally written, "Tchk! Tchk!" She shook her head.

"What am I going to do?" Lisa–Cinderella asked.

"You shouldn't have interfered. It doesn't do to meddle with stories that everyone has known for years," her godmother said.

"I know. I'm sorry."

"I don't know why you think you know better than anyone else what ought to happen."

"I said I was sorry," poor Lisa said.

"If you didn't lose a shoe, then the Prince has nothing to help him find you."

"Couldn't you magic another shoe for him

to find?" Lisa asked.

"Do you want him to go around looking for a lady with three feet?" her godmother asked.

"There must be some sort of magic that you could do," Lisa said.

"I could turn you into a rat. Until midnight, of course," her godmother said.

"I don't see how that would help," Lisa said.

"If you were a rat, you could get into the palace without anyone seeing you. At midnight you'd change back into yourself. You might be able to persuade the Prince that you were the beautiful stranger."

"When I look like this? And when he'd seen

me first as a rat?'' Lisa asked.

The fairy godmother was just about to make a huffy reply, when there was a tremendous banging on the front door. The voice of the Prince's herald rang out. "Any unmarried girls in this house? The Prince wishes to see

any such young women. He is searching for his future Queen.''

"You'll have to manage this for yourself,'' the fairy godmother said nastily, and vanished just as the door opened and the royal party were ushered in. Lisa–Cinderella's stepmother was horrified that they had walked straight into the kitchen, but the Prince, who was doing the job very thoroughly and had already visited over a hundred houses where there were known to be unmarried girls, refused to move. He sat on a kitchen chair and asked to see the daughters of the family.

After a short pause, the ugliest sister appeared. She curtsied to the Prince, then came forward and lifted the hem of her skirt to show that she was wearing golden boots, laced high to the knee. She looked very pleased with herself. She was sure she had guessed what sort of footwear the Prince was looking for. She meant to be the next Queen.

"No thank you. Take her away," the Prince said after one horrified glance.

"Look at me! I am Twinkletoes, the bal-lerina!" the plain sister sang out as she came pirouetting into the room in a pair of silver ballet shoes.

"It's not her. Any other girls in the house?" the Prince asked, preparing to move on next door.

Lisa had had time to run upstairs to collect the glass slippers. Now she approached the

Prince and held the slippers out towards him. "I've got these," she said, not sure whether she should put the slippers on herself, or wait for him to fit the first one as the real Cinderella had done.

The Prince looked at her doubtfully. Then he looked again, first at her face and then at the slippers. Then he said, "Yes. You don't look exactly as you did the other night, but I recognize you in spite of that. You are the unknown beauty at the ball, and my be-

trothed bride. You and I will now go back to the palace to prepare for our marriage, which will take place as soon as possible, if you agree."

"That turned out better than I'd expected," the fairy godmother said, appearing beside the Prince so suddenly that she made him jump. She took out her wand. "And now, my dear, you *shall* go to the b . . . I mean, of course, you shall marry the Prince and live happily ever after. But not in those clothes." She touched Lisa's rags with her wand, and there was a shimmering ball gown again.

The godmother shook her head.

"Not quite right for a morning visit to future relatives," she said, and with another

flourish of the wand she had changed the ball gown into a deliciously stylish suit of dark green velvet, with a little tricorne hat to match.

Lisa bent down to put on the glass slippers. The Prince held out his hand for them.

"Allow me," he said. But instead of fitting them on Lisa-Cinderella's feet, he tucked them under his arm. "A souvenir of our first meeting," he said, and the fairy godmother, smiling benignly, just had time to cover Lisa's bare feet with a neat pair of green satin pumps, before she vanished as suddenly as she had appeared.

"How did you know that I was wearing glass slippers?" Lisa asked the Prince, when

they were alone in his chariot, riding towards the palace.

"My lovely girl! At the ball, you looked wonderful. Your manners were perfect, and your conversation was fascinating. But your dancing . . .! If you'll forgive my saying so, it was like partnering a hippopotamus with iron feet. In our first minuet, you had kicked me twice and trodden on my toes four times.

After our quadrille, I was black and blue from the knee to the toes. I realized that you must be wearing shoes made of something extremely unyielding. Certainly not leather or silk. So when I set out to find you, all I had to look for was a girl with a very unusual type of footwear."

"I'm very sorry," Lisa said.

"Don't apologize. If you'd been a better dancer, I might never have guessed how to track you down," the Prince said, hugging her affectionately. Lisa hugged him back. He really was very handsome. But she wasn't thinking only about the Prince. She was wondering if perhaps her godmother had been right. Things are apt to get very complicated when you start interfering with the way a well-known story has always been told.

Alison Uttley
Foxglove Tales £1.95

Nowhere is Alison Uttley's magical blend of fantasy, humour and feeling for nature more apparent than in this delightful collection of twelve of her very best stories. Five of them come from her first book, *Moonshine and Magic*, and the three from her last, *Lavender Shoes*, reveal that she had lost none of her skill at the age of eighty-six! Sam Pig and Tim Rabbit, two of her most popular heroes, are represented, and there are stories from *Nine Starlight Tales* and *The Weathercock*. Altogether, a classic to treasure.

Alison Uttley's *Tales of Little Grey Rabbit* and *Tales of Little Brown Field Mouse* are also available in Piccolo.

Rudyard Kipling
Just So Stories £1.95

How the Elephant's Child had his nose pulled by the Crocodile; how the Rhinoceros got his skin and a very bad temper; how the Leopard, in a spot, took the Wise Bavarian's advice and got spots . . .

The *Just So Stories*, originally told to his daughter, are among Kipling's finest. Witty and inventive, with illustrations full of hidden jokes and puzzles by the author himself, they will be much appreciated when read aloud to younger children.

Rewards and Fairies £2.50

Like *Puck of Pook's Hill*, this book takes as its theme the story of the Land and its People throughout time. Once again, Puck guides the children, Dan and Una, through the great dramas of history. But the true hero of the book is Hobden, the old yeoman, who instinctively understands the whole story of the Land, for he himself is part of its life and tradition . . .

Joan Aiken
Fog Hounds, Wind Cat, Sea Mice £1.75

The Fog Hounds were silent, mysterious – and deadly. They belonged to the King and they roamed all over the land from dusk to dawn. No-one who had been chased by them ever lived to tell the tale. But Tad was not afraid of them. He even wanted to own one . . .

Tad's adventure is the first in this masterly collection specially written to bridge the gap between first picture books and longer stories.

All these books are available at your local bookshop or newsagent, or can be ordered direct from the publisher. Indicate the number of copies required and fill in the form below

....

Name ———————————————————————————————————
(Block letters please)

Address————————————————————————————————————

——

Send to CS Department, Pan Books Ltd,
PO Box 40, Basingstoke, Hants
Please enclose remittance to the value of the cover price plus:
35p for the first book plus 15p per copy for each additional book
ordered to a maximum charge of £1.25 to cover postage and
packing
Applicable only in the UK

While every effort is made to keep prices low, it is sometimes necessary to increase prices at short notice. Pan Books reserve the right to show on covers and charge new retail prices which may differ from those advertised in the text or elsewhere